Tex

Tex

Story by Myrelene Ranville
Illustrations by Clive Dobson

FIREFLY BOOKS

A FIREFLY BOOK

Published in Canada in 1999 by
Firefly Books Ltd.
3680 Victoria Park Avenue
Willowdale, Ontario, Canada
M2H 3K1

Published in the United States in 1999 by
Firefly Books (U.S.) Inc.
P.O. Box 1338, Ellicott Station
Buffalo, New York, USA
14205

Cataloguing in Publication Data

Ranville, Myrelene
  Tex
ISBN 1-55209-294-1 (bound)   ISBN 1-55209-291-7 (pbk.)
I. Dobson, Clive, 1949- . II. Title.
PS8585.A59T49 1998   jC813'.54   C98-930991-6
PZ7.R177Te 1998

Design by Joseph Gisini / Andrew Smith Graphics Inc.
Film work by Rainbow Digicolor Inc., Toronto
Printed and bound in Canada by Friesens, Altona, Manitoba

*The publishers acknowledge the financial support of the Government
of Canada through the Book Publishing Industry Development Program
for our publishing activities.*

First Printing

Are you wondering why
Tex was in the dog pound?

Tex was the smallest of eight English Foxhound puppies. When the puppies were young all they did was eat and sleep. For six weeks after they were born, their mother fed the hungry little Foxhounds enough milk to make them grow strong and healthy. All the puppies looked like they would grow to be champion show dogs, but not Tex. He was too small. When people say the runt of the litter, they mean the littlest puppy, like Tex.

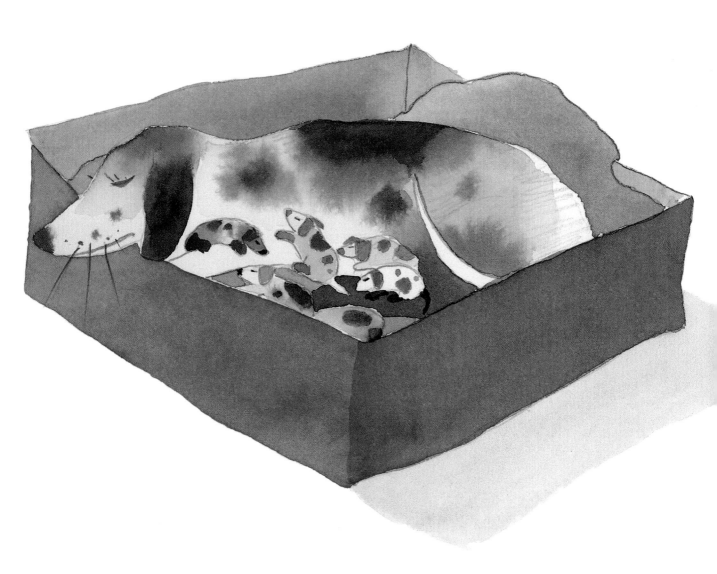

The puppies grew very fast. They were able to walk in only two weeks. As soon as they were able, they would play, rolling over each other, nipping at tails and ears, and gnawing on the edge of the big red box. Tex thought his brothers and sisters looked just like him. They all had lots of white hair and black spots and all eight puppies lived happily in a big red box with their mother.

Soon the puppies were being examined and checked by the veterinarian. Each little dog was examined from its ears to the tip of its tail. As he worked, the veterinarian made check marks and X's in his book.

Then the puppy experts began to visit each day. They all carried books that told them which puppies might grow up to become champions. The puppies were checked to see if they matched the champion dogs shown in the puppy expert book. The black hair spots could be different in shape but their bodies had to be exactly as the book described. The puppy experts also made check marks and X's in their books.

In Tex's house, there was another important book. This was the Champion Record Book. It contained the names of all the dogs that had lived in the big red box and had grown to become champions. They had names like Sir Galahad, Missy, Sir Byron, Sweet Catherine, and many more. Would one of this litter someday become a champion?

Soon, other people began to come to see the puppies in the big red box. Since the puppies were English Foxhounds, they understood what the people were saying in English. They said things like, "I would like this one," picking up a puppy.

It seemed like every time the puppies heard the words, "I like this one," there would be one puppy fewer in the big red box. Tex didn't know why some of the puppies were leaving the box. He didn't know they would not be coming back. Every day the box seemed to have more room, and Tex's mother had more milk for the remaining puppies to drink. Tex liked the extra room.

When the puppies could eat solid food, Tex's mother was taken to live in another box. Only Tex and his two sisters were left in the big red box. Tex thought that they would continue to live there all their lives.

The puppies listened to stories about dog shows coming up in cities far from Tex's home. One day, Tex heard something about the dog pound.

The woman who owned Tex's mother said, "If no one asks to take Tex, he will have to go to the dog pound." People did not ask for Tex because he had an overbite. He thought he had better be careful not to bite too much. He didn't want to show his overbite.

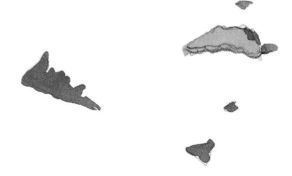

One day, Tex was taken from the big red box. "Someone has asked for me!" Tex thought. But no one had asked for Tex. Instead, he was taken out of the house and put into a cage in a car. Tex was still very small. He couldn't stand up in the moving car, and he was very scared. When the car stopped, Tex noticed he had left a puddle.

The woman who owned Tex's mother said, "Tex, this is the dog pound. You will live here now. Good bye, Tex."

Then she left.

Tex was put in a wire cage. It was all very strange. He heard different noises, smelled different smells. There were dogs Tex didn't know in cages all around him. Each dog made a different sound. Tex could not understand them. Some little dogs made very sharp sounds. Some of the big dogs made gruff, loud sounds. All of the dogs Tex had known before had made the same sounds. They all had voices like his own.

Now nothing was the same.

Tex was lonely. But one of the people at the dog pound was very kind and said to him, "Someone will fall in love with you and take you home."

One day, Tex heard someone say, "Yes, we do have a puppy with a good temperament. He does not even try to bite. He is a very smart dog. If he didn't have an overbite, he would be in a big city dog show right now." Tex knew that they were talking about him! He quickly remembered why he did not care to be a show dog. Tex had heard stories about the life a show dog leads. Airplane flying and car riding in wire cages was not for him.

He wanted a dog's life! He wanted to live in a nice loving home, and he needed to be someone's friend.

Tex saw a woman walking toward him. She looked so brown and healthy. She seemed to have just come in from the hot sun. She said to Tex: "*Aneen, Animoosh. Neen Anishnabay Ikwe.*" Which means, in her native language, "How are you, dog? I am Ikwe, an Anishnabay woman."

Tex was taken out of the cage and handed to Ikwe. She cuddled him and said, "I would like to be your best friend. We will share a home." Then Ikwe said to the woman who runs the dog pound, "*Mee ahway!* This is the one! He is perfect. I would like to take him home with me and I will love him. Does he have a name?" "His name is Tex," she was told. "I like his name," Ikwe said. "*Abay ohma*, Tex."

Tex leaped into her arms!

So now you know why Tex was in the dog pound, and how he came to live with Ikwe and be her *Animoosh* – her dog.

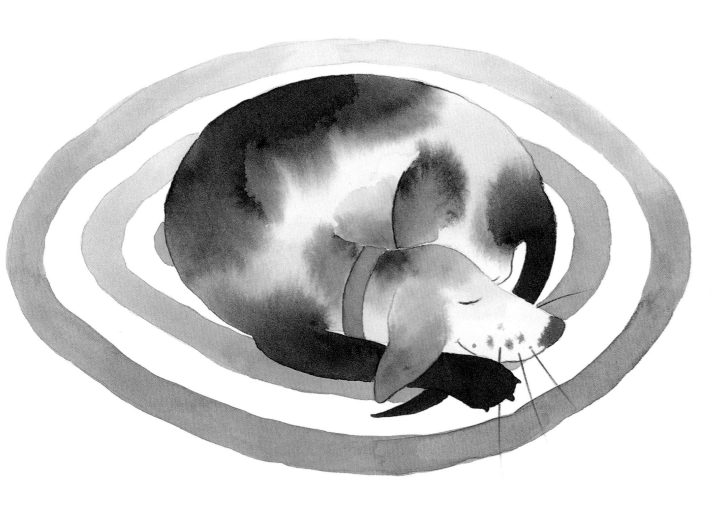